the world's GREATEST underachiever

# HankZIPZER

## THE BALLOT BOX BRAWL

### THEO BAKER

**WALKER**
ENTERTAINMENT

First published in Great Britain 2016 by Walker Entertainment, an imprint of Walker Books Ltd, 87 Vauxhall Walk, London SE11 5HJ

Based on the television series "Hank Zipzer" produced by Kindle Entertainment in association with DHX Media Ltd. Based on the screenplay *Camouflage*. Reproductions © 2014 Hank Zipzer Productions Limited

2 4 6 8 10 9 7 5 3 1

Text © 2016 Walker Books Ltd
Cover by Walker Books Ltd

This book has been typeset in OpenDyslexic

Printed and bound in Great Britain by Clays Ltd, St Ives plc

British Library Cataloguing in Publication Data:
a catalogue record for this book is available from the British Library

ISBN 978-1-4063-6791-1

www.walker.co.uk

the world's GREATEST underachiever

# HankZipzer

**Hank Zipzer the World's
Greatest Underachiever series
by Henry Winkler and Lin Oliver**

This book has been set in OpenDyslexic –
a font which has been created
to increase readability for readers
with dyslexia. The font is continually
being updated and improved,
based on input from dyslexic users.

# CHAPTER ONE

The worst part about Monday is that the day actually starts on Sunday morning, right in the middle of breakfast. That's when it hits me: I have school tomorrow!

After that, I can't eat another bite. It might as well be Monday. All I can think about is school, how much I don't want to go, and all the homework I've got to do, which I should have done on Friday, or Saturday, so I could do something cool on Sunday – like laser tag. Or play Digging for Gold on my computer, the most addictive game in the known universe. It's a really simple game. All you do is cruise around the beach and dig little holes. But sometimes there's gold in those holes, and when there is, the game plays this sound effect of clinking gold coins, and man do I love that sound. You use the gold to upgrade your shovel, and the more upgraded your shovel is (mine is the fourth most powerful shovel in the game), the more holes you can dig, and thar be gold in some of them holes.

But I never get to play Digging for Gold on Sunday. My dad fixed that. One day while I was out he got deep into my computer and installed all these parental controls and focusing apps so that the only things I can access on Sunday, from 9.30 a.m. to 11.59 p.m., are Word and Math Miners, a game where you get brass ingots for solving incredibly complex maths problems in the Cave of Integers. It's ... well, let's just say it's no Digging for Gold.

So now I spend my Sundays in front of my computer, either trying to delete all the parental controls my dad installed, or just looking at a blank document screen, feeling doom in my stomach. Then it's time to go to bed.

Last year, I could fall asleep on Sunday night thinking about tacos. But they took that away too. Over the summer my school hired one of those health-nut chefs to overhaul the cafeteria menu. And the first thing Chef Anton did was to get rid of Taco Mondays. Now we have a lovely "roasted fennel and shaved mushroom medley" on Mondays, and no dessert. Maybe that tastes decent in the chef's restaurant, but the Westbrook Academy cafeteria staff aren't up to the challenge.

I guess the only thing Monday has going for it is that there's a school-wide assembly first thing in the morning. Everyone else hates it, but I say what's to hate? I mean, it's better than class with Miss Adolf. All you have to do is sit there and breathe. No one's yelling at you. No one's barking at you to tuck in your shirt or stay in line. No one's making you solve maths problems or forcing you to read a story about Philip and Jules and which of them gets to Essex first at different starting times and speeds.

You don't even have to smile or pretend to be interested in whatever's happening up at the lectern. You're allowed to be exactly what you are: sleepy and bored. Monday morning assemblies are like a giant snooze button for the week.

And the best part about the assemblies is that our new head teacher, Mr Joy, really adores the sound of his own voice. He talks and talks, loving every minute of it, and so do I. Sometimes he evens blows right through all of first lesson and keeps on going into second lesson. And so while I'm zoning out during the assembly, I let myself

dream that he'll just keep talking until it's
Friday, or Miss Adolf retires, or they let me
graduate because enough years have gone
by.

# CHAPTER TWO

Someone elbows my shoulder.

"Whhzzm?!" I sputtered.

"This is bad," my best mate Frankie said.

"Really bad," said my other best friend, Ashley.

"... speeches for the election are this Thursday, followed by a vote. Anyone who wants to take part should sign up with Miss Adolf after assembly..."

"Wake up, Hank," Frankie said and elbowed me again. I was mostly asleep, even though my eyes were open.

"Your sister is running for the vacant seat on school council. She just raised her hand."

"And so is Nick McKelty," Ashley added.

"Nine more minutes," I mumbled, and fell mostly back asleep, the words "McKelty" and "school council" doing a dream dance in my brain. I saw Nick McKelty standing in front of Mr Joy's desk, his hair smoothed back, wearing a slick politician's suit with a sash that read "World President".

"Go on, Hank," Dream-President McKelty was saying, pointing at his polished shoes. "Kiss them."

"But—" I started.

"Would you rather detention?" Dream-Miss Adolf said. She was lurking in the shadowy corner of President McKelty's office, gripping an evil sorcerer's staff. "Now kiss your president's shoes," she said and raised her staff. And though every muscle in my dream body resisted, I felt myself

13

getting to my knees, lowering my head, and puckering up...

"YUCK!" I yelled and jerked forward, now wide awake. Everyone in assembly turned back and stared at me, and it was like the crowd parted so Mr Joy could look right at me from the lectern.

"Mr Zipzer, I won't have you insulting Chef Anton and his staff," Mr Joy said. "They've worked tirelessly to provide you with healthy, farm-fresh creations. Give their menu a chance, and in time, I'm certain you'll come to appreciate gravlax."

"Oh no, I love gravlax!" I said, automatically. What was I saying? Mr Joy and every other single kid in Westbrook Academy were looking at me. "It's gravaliscious."

"Indeed it is," Mr Joy said. "In fact, I could go for some right now. Dismissed!"

While everyone got up and started filing out, I stayed sitting. Mostly because I was

14

still partly asleep, and a little bit because
a fantastic idea was coming together in my
dream brain.

"I don't understand why they want to be
on school council," Frankie said, motioning
towards Emily and McKelty, who were
standing with Miss Adolf.

"Because they want power," Ashley said.

"We can't let McKelty get power," I said.
"He'll make us kiss his shoes."

"Rise and shine, Hank," Frankie said, and
elbowed me again.

"I'm awake! And I'm running for world
president!" I leapt to my feet and threw up
my arms.

"It's just student council," Ashley said,
"but I think it's a great idea."

"I'll be your campaign manager," Frankie
said.

"And I'll be your chief campaign
strategist," Ashley said.

"Actually, this is starting to sound like a

lot of work," I said, and sat back down.

"No, no, Hank!" Ashley said. "It's your destiny to be on the school council."

"And to do whatever it takes to keep McKelty from having power over us," Frankie said. "All in favour of Hank running for school council say 'Aye'."

He and Ashley both raised their hands and said "Aye".

"The 'ayes' have it," Ashley said. "Congrats, Hank. We've nominated you."

"Wait, don't I get a vote?" I asked.

"Sure, but it wouldn't matter," Frankie said. "It's two against one. Majority rules."

"I'm not sure if I like politics," I said, putting on a kingly kind of voice. "But if the people have spoken, I shall obey. The greater good calls to me, to Hank, your leader, your saviour. I am Hank, crusher of McKelty, hero of Westbrook Academy, president of the world!"

# CHAPTER THREE

By "Nutrition by Chef Anton" time –
formerly known as "mid-morning break" – I
started to think that perhaps politics wasn't
going to be all fun and games; instead
of trying to eat a selection of dried figs
garnished with seasonal watercress, I had
to go and sign up for this school council
election. And that meant going to the most
haunted place in all of Westbrook Academy:
*the staffroom!*

But the greater good was calling me.
There was no way I could stand by as

McKelty – or Emily – grabbed the reins of power, even if it meant going across enemy lines. I put my head down and charged towards my destiny. My momentum sent me right through the double doors, and I didn't stop until I was standing directly in front of Miss Adolf.

She finished drawing a red frowny face on a worksheet and looked up at me with raised eyebrows. I sort of frowned and smiled at her at the same time. Then I looked down and stuffed my hands into my pockets.

"A word on manners, Henry," Miss Adolf said. "It's impolite to burst into the staffroom and then stand there with an inscrutable expression."

"I, uh, want to stand for school council."

"What a wonderful idea, Hank," Mr Rock said from another table. He's the music teacher, and pretty much my only grown-up ally anywhere in Westbrook Academy. He was re-stringing the school's electric guitar. "I think you'll make a great school councillor. You have so much compassion."

"No," Miss Adolf said, and drew two more frowny faces on some poor kid's worksheet, which was covered in blood-red "X"s. Then she wrote "See me!" on top, right next to the poor kid's name. That poor kid had the same name as me.

"What do you mean, "no"?" Mr Rock asked. He'd finished stringing the guitar and had started tuning it.

"Putting aside my own personal feelings on the inadequacies of democracy," Miss Adolf said, "the headmaster said everyone was to sign up by the *end* of assembly."

"No he didn't," Mr Rock said. "Mr Joy said that students can sign up *after* assembly." He glanced at his watch, and held it up to Miss Adolf. "As you can see, it's after assembly."

"That's *not* what he meant."

"Yeah, but that's what he said."

Just then, Mr Joy himself came into the staffroom carrying a white take-away food carton. Miss Adolf went straight to him and told him all about the dispute. He listened with his hand on his chin. "I think we can make an exception for a fellow gravlax lover," Mr Joy said, giving me a wink before walking to the furthest table to sit down.

"Congratulations, Mr Zipzer," Miss Adolf said through her teeth as she returned to her seat. She took out the sign-up sheet and wrote my name so hard that she broke the pen's point. A huge glob of red ink pooled around my name. "You're now officially a candidate for school council."

"All right!" Mr Rock shouted, and strummed a power chord on the guitar. Then he played one of those cheesy riffs that guitar guys always play when they want to show off.

"No music in the staffroom," Miss Adolf growled. "Didn't you see the sign?"

"I saw your sign," he said. "But did you see mine?" He pointed to a hand-decorated sign over the coffee machine that read: "Follow Your Dream!"

As Miss Adolf and Mr Rock started arguing about whose sign held greater authority, I saw my chance to get as far from the staffroom as possible. I lowered my eyes, dropped my shoulders, and was all set to slink away at warp speed when Mr Joy called out to me.

"Oh, Henry? Won't you join me a moment?"

"Er ... sure..." I said, eyeing the door and rifling through my bag, trying to give the impression that I had somewhere school-related to get to.

"Have a seat," he said, and tapped the white take-away box. "I had the cafeteria whip up tomorrow's lunch for me. That's one of the perks of being the boss. As a fellow lover of gravlax, I thought you'd appreciate a little treat."

"Huh?"

Mr Joy opened the box. There was a mound of some sort of flesh that was a colour somewhere between pink and orange. "Sit! Sit! There's more than enough for two."

Another reason I try to stay as far as possible from the staffroom is that there's always a chance I'll see one of the teachers eating. I don't like to see teachers eating. It kind of weirds me out.

I had nothing to talk about with Mr Joy except for gravlax. I wanted to ask what kind of animal or plant gravlax came from, but then he'd know I lied about loving it. Instead, I told him that my grandpa, Papa Pete, had been making me gravlax since I was in nappies. He made it every Sunday, I said. And when there was something really sensitive I needed to talk about, Papa Pete made his famous gravlax and we talked about all my problems over gravlax. I was really on a gravlax roll. I even said that gravlax was the speciality at our family's deli, the Spicy Salami.

"Why did he name it the Spicy Salami then?"

I leaned in close. "For political reasons."

"I see," Mr Joy said. Then he leaned in close, too. "Listen, Henry. I want to bring you in on something. Do I have your confidence?"

I told him that he did. Why not?

"Well, Henry, this has to be kept on the hush-hush, but the new menu has been getting lots of complaints. Kids aren't eating, they're withering away. Parents are writing letters to the school board. The cafeteria staff are threatening to strike. It's just a mess."

Then he sighed and kind of stared off. He seemed to be waiting for me to offer my help.

"But there is something you can do,

Henry," he finally said. "Once you're elected to the school council, I want you to use your position to promote the new menu. Tell all your mates about the importance of a healthy, farm-fresh diet. I'd like you to work with me on this, Henry. I am a man who knows how to return a favour," Mr Joy paused to press his chest, and let out a silent belch. "Do we have a deal?"

"I, uh…" I paused to think. This had got really weird, really fast.

"You play your cards close, don't you, Mr Zipzer?" Mr Joy said. "Good man. You're a natural-born politician."

"Uh, thanks?"

"I've got to be running now." Mr Joy got up and straightened his tie. "I'll leave the rest of this gravlax for you to enjoy at your leisure. A taste of things to come."

After Mr Joy left, I sat there trying to figure out what had just happened. Mr Rock plopped himself down in the chair across from me.

"I think Mr Joy just tried to bribe me with gravlax," I told him.

Mr Rock leaned in for a sniff of the box and jerked back in disgust. "Hey, that's politics."

# CHAPTER FOUR

The rest of Monday went great. Word
got around that I was standing for school
council, and a few kids came up to me and
said that I had their vote. "I'll vote for
anyone but McKelty," one of them said. I
considered that a compliment. Really, I felt
a good vibe at school. I felt like everyone
wanted to vote for me. And why not? I'd
vote for me.

I couldn't lose.

I wasn't sure about everything that had
happened with Mr Joy, but one thing was

certain: I wanted to be on the school council. I could be a force for good. I could get rid of the new healthy menu and bring back Taco Mondays. I could also start half-day Tuesdays, no-test Wednesdays, and no-homework Everydays.

There were so many great things I could accomplish with just a little power. And even if I didn't feel like doing any of those things and just sort of coasted, I would still be a force for good. Both McKelty and my little sister would do evil and strange things, and make everyone's life worse. At least I wouldn't make anything worse, and for that the people would love me!

I was thinking about the school's fantastic future as I walked home with Frankie and Ashley. But they kept trying to pull my head out of the clouds and bring me down to their anxious, earth-bound level.

"But you have to get elected first," Frankie said.

"And it won't be easy," Ashley added.

"Sure it will," I told them. "Nobody wants to vote for McKelty. And I'm pretty sure that nobody even knows who Emily is."

"But you have to mount a campaign," Ashley said.

"So I'll make a few posters that say 'Vote Hank. He's not McKelty', and hey presto." I flashed my hands with a magician's flourish.

My mates were not impressed.

"He doesn't have a chance," Ashley said to Frankie.

"What's the big deal, guys?" I said. "McKelty has, like, zero friends. I'm a dead cert"

"This is politics, Hank," Frankie said.

"And this is McKelty," Ashley echoed. "It doesn't matter if nobody likes him. That's not the point."

"McKelty's not going to fight fair," Frankie said. "He's going to spread rumours about you. He's going to disrupt your operations. He's going to hack into your computer. He's going to dig deep into your past."

"Not my past!" I exclaimed, holding the back of my hand up to my forehead.

"By the time he's done with you," Ashley said. "Your name will be a bad word. That's right, he's going to smear your good name."

"Not my good name!" I cried, swooning with my other hand.

"Hey Ashley, can I talk to you for a moment over here?" Frankie asked.

"Absolutely."

The two sauntered about fifteen feet away and huddled together for a secret conversation, glancing my way every now and then and shaking their heads.

"Hey! Look, guys," I shouted. "There goes a dog wearing a sweater! He's got shoes on too. He's over here! Hallooooo..."

But they didn't look. They totally froze

me out. When they were done with their obnoxiously private little conversation, they came back and stood facing me.

"Hank, as your trusted aides," Frankie announced, "we've decided that we're resigning unless we all meet tonight to discuss campaign strategy."

"I appreciate your feedback," I said. "And as the head of this campaign, I am grateful for your commitment and dedication. In fact, I'm going to reward you, by giving both of you the night off."

Ashley frowned. "Do you really want McKelty to be elected? 'Cos that's what it seems like."

"Listen guys," I said, putting my foot down. "It's my name on the ballot, so I need to do this my way. I'll take care of McKelty, no problem. But if you guys really think it necessary, we can meet *tomorrow* night and do campaign stuff. Tonight, I just want to relax and play Digging for Gold for about six hours. I haven't played since Saturday and my hands are starting to shake. Also, my throat is feeling dry. But that might be unrelated."

Both of them just glared at me.

"But if you two want to meet to discuss campaign strategy on your own, you have my full support."

# CHAPTER FIVE

I burst into the flat, all smiles, ready for a Digging for Gold marathon. I let my bag fall from my shoulders, and went to the kitchen for a giant Thermos of orange juice and an economy size bag of crisps, so the only thing that would interrupt my gaming would be nature's call.

Emily was already at home, sitting at the dinner table in front of her laptop and about a dozen neatly organized binders.

"Looks like we'll be running against each other," I said. "May the best man win."

"To win in politics, you have to be politically correct," she said. "I use inclusive, gender-neutral nomenclature. May the best *humanoid* win."

I wasn't sure if she was joking or not. It's hard to tell with Emily. She was just looking at me with her beady eyes, and her usual blank expression. So I stuck out my hand, thinking we could shake on a clean, hard-fought contest. She didn't even glance at it.

"Well," I said. "Nice talk, sis. I'm off to play Digging for Gold."

"You're not going to work on your campaign?"

"It's all up here," I said, and tapped my noggin.

"You've already come up with your platform?" she asked.

"Let me check," I said. "Um, brain, have we—"

"What about your slogan? Or polling data? Demographic breakdowns? Campaign literature? Direct-mailing lists? Poster design?"

"Uh—"

"You haven't even figured out where you're going to print your posters? You wouldn't want to print them out at home. They should be done at a professional printer's."

"My staff are handling all those minor details."

"Hank, unless you approach this campaign with seriousness and rigour, you're going to suffer a humiliating defeat. As in, you'll lose to McKelty by a landslide. And for someone like you, whose sense of self-worth comes from how much other people like you, a loss to McKelty won't just be a political loss, but you'll lose your entire sense of identity. You'll be crushed. It could take years for you to recover."

"Really?"

"Certainly," she said. She opened up

one of her binders and took out a sheet of paper, and gave it to me. "Here's something I've prepared for you."

The paper was a checklist of all the things Emily thought I needed to do to win the election. In typical Emily fashion, it was quite detailed. She'd scheduled my next three days down to the minute.

"Thanks, sis," I said. "You did a lot of work for me— waiiit. Why did you do all this work for me?"

"That's my campaign strategy," she said. "In order for me to win, I need you and McKelty to go after each other and attack until everyone is so fed up with the election that they vote for me."

"But now that I know that," I said, trying to read all the different ways Emily was going to sabotage me, "I can stop it from happening, right?"

"Wrong," she said. "If you follow my programme, I win, but you still get more votes than McKelty. If you don't follow the programme, McKelty wins the seat. This is political science. Mathematics. The truth is in the numbers. See? I've plotted it on a graph."

Everything went hazy there for a moment. I heard my heart beating. I felt sweat rolling down my cheeks.

Then I snapped out of it. "Nah," I said, and crumpled up the paper. "This is McKelty. Everyone thinks he's lame. And everyone will vote for me, because everyone knows I'm amazing. Nice try, humanoid."

I patted Emily on the head. Then I went to my room, fired up the old PC, clicked a couple of buttons, and heard the soothing, rotating music from Digging for Gold.

"Rrrrr, matey," the computer said. "Are ye ready?!"

"Aye, aye, cap'n!"

"Then get ye ready to dig. And remember, matey, thar be gold in some of them holes!"

I started digging. The gold was flowing. My little guy cruised around the beach with his super-upgraded shovel, digging hole after hole. I just sort of zoned out, looking at the computer-world sky, with those puffy clouds going by. I thought nothing. Everything in my world was easy and nice.

And then, from out of nowhere, it hit me: what if I really did lose?

Emily was right. It was totally possible that McKelty could win. And then, not only would he be on the school council, but it would be all my fault. And for ever after, I would be remembered as the guy who lost to Nick McKelty! I would probably win. But there was always a chance I could lose. Especially if McKelty was playing dirty. I needed to make certain that I would win; my reputation was at stake. I had to get a ton of people to vote for me. A ton. This was no game.

Then all my anxiety went away when my little guy struck gold, and I heard the coins clinking. I'd reached 10,000 "pieces o' eight" – gold coins – and I had enough to upgrade to Feung's Legacy, the *third* best shovel in the game. It had three separate blades on it, so every time you dug, you made three holes. I dug up that whole beach in lightning speed, just smiling, until WHAM!

I had an amazing idea!

I grabbed a yellow pad and started sketching like crazy.

# CHAPTER SIX

**From the electronic files of the Elect Emily Zipzer campaign:**

Campaign Statement:

My campaign is based on ideas, and the optimization of those ideas. If the voters study my ideas carefully, then they will find that the ideas are entirely correct.

Campaign Platform:

Plank 1: Lengthen the school day.

Plank 2: Install a terrarium sanctuary in

the school cafeteria a dedicated oasis for all of London's abandoned lizards.

Plank 3: No excessive noise. Students must dedicate their day to quiet study at their desks. During a fifteen minute break, students may make some enthusiastic vocalizations.

Plank 4: No unstructured play during break time. Students may participate in one of four educational games which teach a scholastic lesson. If students do not wish to participate, they may read quietly at their desks, or volunteer at the lizard sanctuary.

Plank 5: Students will be required to input their educational goals into an electronic database, and then they must enter hourly updates as to how they are, or are not, achieving those goals.

Campaign Strategy:
The strength of my campaign lies in the strength of my ideas. Looking over my

platform, however, I'm certain of one thing: my ideas will not be immediately popular. This might be a surmountable obstacle if I were popular, but I am not popular.

So during lunchtime today, I went to the library. To my surprise, the Westbrook Academy library had scant material about how British become popular, and what little material I did find was horrifically out of date. I decided that I would have to conduct my own primary investigation on popularity, and then use the results to bolster my campaign.

At the very least, I could perhaps publish my findings in a scientific journal.

I wonder if publishing in a scientific journal makes one popular? My scientific instincts tell me it would.

# CHAPTER SEVEN

I stayed at my desk, sketching so much that my hand was throbbing, until Mum called us for dinner. I jogged over and left my pad on the table while I went to help Mum carry the hot stuff from the oven to the table. That's my unofficial dinnertime job, by the way: carrying the hot stuff. It's better than washing the dishes, and I get to say "Watch out, hot stuff coming through!" every night. It never gets old – at least not for me and Dad.

While I was busy risking my skin for

dinner, Emily stole a peek at my notepad.

"Is this the design for your poster?" she asked. "It's quite ... different."

"Watch out, hot stuff coming through!" Dad squealed a high-pitched little laugh from the bedroom.

I plopped the meat loaf on the placemat and turned my attention to Emily, who looked sceptical. "That, dear Emily, is the answer to all my problems."

"Expand on that."

"Gladly," I said, snatching back the pad and taking a long sip of water. "First, I want to ask you a question. What's the hardest part about getting elected?" Emily opened her mouth to answer, but I cut her off. "That's right, getting enough votes. You run your campaign, but you can never be sure you'll get enough votes. But this little baby solves that. I present to you the 'Vote-inator', a modern voting device for our modern age. This fantastic contraption lets you vote ten times at once. When you're using this trademarked invention, you can be certain of victory. Like it?"

I admired the sketches a moment. They had lots of sprockets and mechanical arms.

"I got the idea from my video game," I added. "And everyone's always saying that you can't learn anything from video games!"

"I'm certain that your game is making you measurably stupider every time you play it."

"So you think it's great?"

"Yes, Hank. You've just revolutionized electoral fraud."

"What's all this talk about elections?" Mum asked as she brought over the salad.

"We're each running for school council," Emily told her. "Against McKelty."

"Oh, um, OK..." Mum said, and portioned out the salad while continuing to mumble.

I was still looking at the sketches of my Vote-inator. It really looked cool. Like one of those machines from old cartoons.

Honestly, I knew about halfway through the afternoon that my Vote-inator wasn't a realistic idea, but it was better than thinking about losing to McKelty.

"Isn't this great, love," Dad said as he plopped himself down. "Both our kids are running for elected office, just like their old dad did. We'll be a political dynasty!"

"I always thought you had to get elected to be in a political dynasty," Mum said, smiling to herself.

"No, love, you can come in third, and do it honourably. Yup, it was a very strong third place showing." Dad sliced off the end piece of meat loaf and served himself. He turned to Emily and me. "I ran for secretary of my university's crossword club."

"And how many voting members were there in your club?" Mum asked.

"Several. It was a fierce competition among the finest mates I've ever had the pleasure to know," Dad said, with a faraway look in his eyes. Mum rolled her eyes.

It took a moment, but he snapped out of it. "You see, kids, I know a lot about sports," he said. "And more often than not, the best coaches were not star players in their playing days. To be an effective coach, you need to stand outside the game a bit. Get a feel for the big picture. See how things really work."

Dad paused. It seemed like he was waiting for us all to gasp at his profound thoughts.

"Stan, what are you talking about?"

"Coaching, love. What else would I be talking about? I can coach the kids in their elections, help them smash McKelty. I bet McKelty's dad is helping him. Well, we'll show 'em, won't we, kids? We'll show 'em what it means to be a Zipzer. Let me see what you've got going there, Emily."

"Stan, really. I think—"

He waved "not now" to Mum and then

motioned for Emily to slide her laptop around so he could see the screen. He was clearly confused by what he saw.

"I've been running my latest polling data through some forecasting software," Emily said. "And I've discovered an anomaly."

"Ah, yes, there," he said, pointing at the screen.

"That's the printer icon."

"I mean, there," he said, waving his finger in a wide circle.

"Anyway," Emily said, shutting the laptop, "without an escalated race between McKelty and Hank, the data suggest that I'll only get three votes."

"Well, that's because you need posters. And badges." Dad stood up with a wild gleam in his eye. "I've got some of my old campaign stuff around here somewhere. Love, where's my campaign stuff?"

"Stan, I think it's best if we don't interfere."

"Ah, now I remember!" Dad clapped his hands. "In the cupboard, under my scuba gear."

He started to jog off to the bedroom, but Mum caught him by the shoulder. "Let's have a short chat over here, shall we?"

They stepped a few paces away and started another one of those obnoxiously private little conversations.

"So who are the other two?" I asked Emily.

"Please be more specific."

"The other two votes. You'll vote for yourself, but then who are the other two?"

"Margin of error."

"Never heard of them. Are they in your class?"

Emily sighed. "In statistics, Hank, you're dealing with probabilities. And so you have to— Oh, why am I bothering? Anyway, I don't know what you're so smug about. According to my numbers, you're still losing to McKelty by a landslide. Remember?"

"Let me get a look at those numbers."
I went to grab her laptop, but Emily, with
a movement that I can only describe as
reptilian, pinched my arm and deposited her
laptop into her backpack.

"That's not fair, Em. You got to look at
mine."

Emily shushed me. She was eavesdropping
on Mum and Dad's private conversation.

It wasn't hard to do. They were only six
feet away.

"You know," Mum was saying, "the kids
are growing up. And they need to start
making their own mistakes. We should let
them mess up this election without our
help."

"You know we can hear you, right?" I
said.

# CHAPTER EIGHT

Despite being Gravlax Tuesday, Day One of my campaign started out great. When I woke up, the sun was out, the birds were chirping, and I was sure I'd be a dead cert for the election – no matter what Emily's numbers said.

But things started going downhill during "Nutrition by Chef Anton".

Once again, I couldn't enjoy my nutritious snack, today's being "farfalle balls decorated with aubergine jam". Instead I had to go outside to a roped-off area marked

"ELECTION". Emily was already there, standing under a sign that read, "Vote Emily for Optimized Database Analytics". The only person talking to her was the computer science teacher, Mr Snell, and I'm almost positive he doesn't get to vote.

So I dropped my bag, stood in the middle of the electioneering area and called out, "I'm Hank Zipzer, and I'm running for school council. Come and shake my hand. For free! That's right, free handshakes over here. Come and get your free handshakes!"

It started working almost immediately. An older boy Jesse Winthrop, came over first and gave me a shake. Once everybody saw that it was OK to come and shake my hand, more people joined in. And once I had a crowd going, everyone wanted to get in on the action.

Ashley and Frankie came over about halfway through "Nutrition by Chef Anton".

"Here Hank," Ashley said and placed a

warm, moist thing in my hand. "I brought you a farfalle ball."

"Urgh!" I involuntarily chucked the thing over the crowd of kids vying to shake my presidential hand. I then used the presidential hand to indicate the gathered crowd. "See, guys? I got this. No problem."

"Are you sure that's all you want to do?" Frankie asked. "Shake hands?"

"I'm getting a feel for the student body," I said, giving one kid a shake that blended smoothly into a bear hug. "Look guys, I'm up against Emily and McKelty, not Simone Green or anything."

At that very moment, Simone Green appeared at the edge of the circle around me. She stood with her arms crossed, judging everything her eyes fell on, her little clique of followers watching her every move. Simone Green is the same age as Emily, but she's cooler than a polar bear. I don't know how she does it.

She was watching me, and everyone was watching her to see if she approved of me. I wanted to reach out and give her a handshake, but I couldn't do it. If she rejected my handshake, I'd be humiliated.

After a moment of watching me, she rolled her eyes for all the world to see, and said something like *pfff*. Then, like no one was there, she walked right through my little crowd of supporters.

After that public slight, my mojo started to fade, and my supporters started to peel off.

"If she ran for the student council seat, you wouldn't stand a chance against her," Ashley said. "And I just love her hair accessories."

"She scares me," Frankie said.

"She's cool and all," I said, "but I'm not sweating it. I don't have to beat her, just McKelty. And he's not even here! I bet he chickens out..."

Just then, a siren blared at eardrum-busting levels. And I, turning into some sort of jellyfish, collapsed to the tarmac and cowered behind Ashley's legs. Hardly the stuff of a strong and confident leader.

"Hey, look!" said a girl in Year Eight. "It's McKelty!"

I couldn't see a thing from the ground, through all the shuffling, stomping feet. But I heard plenty. It was McKelty on a loudspeaker.

"Vote McKelty! A name you can trust. What's the name again? McKelty!"

Then it was pandemonium. Kids were throwing up their hands in the air, screaming, shouting, pushing.

"He's giving away sweets!" Frankie shouted.

I looked up to see little sweet packets tumbling through the sky. Outstretched hands were grabbing for the flying confectionery, raining down on the crowd and on my head.

"And he's got a golf cart!" yelled Ashley.

"Nah," I said. But then I got up from the ground. And beyond all the moving, twisting bodies, I saw that my friends weren't lying. McKelty was driving a bright red golf cart. "Pick Nick!" was painted across the side in golden letters.

Kids were losing their minds. This was probably the single coolest thing to ever happen at Westbrook Academy.

I didn't want to be caught gaping, so I dropped back down to one knee and pretended to tie my laces. And from my place on the ground, I saw tyres approaching. They stopped an arm's length away from my head. The crowd parted, and through the crowd came the horn of the loudspeaker, aimed right at me. McKelty winked. "What's that name again?" he blared, right in my eardrum. "McKelty!"

All my supporters were chanting "McKelty!

McKelty!" and they trailed after the golf cart as it scooted away, following the hailstorm of flying sweets. After all was said and done, I was left lying on the ground amid a heap of sweetie wrappers and crushed dreams. Only Ashley and Frankie stayed behind.

"My place, tonight," I said to their told-you-so eyes. "Major brainstorm."

The rest of the day was awful. Everyone in school was talking about McKelty and his golf cart. No one came up to me to say that I had their vote. The only person who came up to me at all was Mr Joy. I was in the cafeteria line, about to be served my gravlax entrée. He came up, put his arm around my shoulder, and told Florence, the cafeteria worker, to "give my mate here two servings".

Florence shrugged, and piled more slop onto my plate. And since Mr Joy stayed to monitor the cafeteria during lunch, I had to eat it all to keep up appearances.

My poor stomach!

# CHAPTER NINE

**From the electronic files of the Elect Emily Zipzer Campaign:**

Campaign Log:

My first day on the campaign trail was a disaster.

I tried, against my better judgement, to run a clean, focused campaign of ideas. I printed out 65 pamphlets that explained my ideas. My ideas were ignored; I still have all 65 pamphlets. It is hard to believe that I could not give away my ideas.

The voters were hungry for other free things, however. Hank gave away free handshakes. McKelty gave away free sweets. Those fickle voters couldn't get enough.

After my disastrous campaign stop during "Nutrition by Chef Anton", I repaired to the library to see if the volume of scholarly essays about popularity I had requested through the inter-library loan system had arrived yet, but the volume was still in transit.

Crestfallen, I left the library, lost in thought. I had two options: change my ideas to more popular ones, or become popular myself. I nearly lost hope. Changing my ideas would be shameful. Without the relevant scientific studies to guide me, becoming popular seemed impossible. I could never ask another kid how to be popular: word would get around that I was *trying* to be popular, and then all hope for success would be lost.

I went to Mr Rock for help; he's the most popular teacher in school. I found him in the assembly hall polishing McKelty's golf cart, which he had just – and justly – confiscated.

I asked a very straightforward question: "How did you become popular?"

He answered with a Zen riddle. "Well, the first thing I do is I *don't* try to be popular," he said.

I nodded, wondering how it was possible to do something by not trying to do it.

"Not everyone's going to love you in this world," he went on, "but if you make one new friend a day, by the end of the year you're going to have a wheelbarrow of Christmas cards."

I didn't want Christmas cards, just votes.

"Just be yourself," he said. "Be authentic. You'll be surprised how many people want to be your friend."

I thanked him for his time. His advice was not helpful, but he had tried, I think. Maybe he was trying to be helpful by not trying?

After my interview with Mr Rock, I roamed the corridors in contemplation.

I was almost ready to go to the staffroom and withdraw my candidacy when I heard inane cackling by the stairs. It was Simone Green and her ridiculous circle of friends. They were sitting on the steps, babbling about boys and shopping. Simone's followers hung on her every word.

*Why is she so popular?* I wondered. She didn't use to be. She used to be a regular girl in my class, just like any other, and then one day, out the blue, she was popular.

I tried to remember what preceded her sudden surge into popularity, and then, with the force of Archimedes' insight about volume displacement in the bath, it hit me. It was all so simple! All that happened was one day in Year Six, Klara Neal was assigned to sit next to Simone Green. At that time Klara was the most popular girl in the class. When Klara had to leave Westbrook suddenly (her father had been transferred to Argentina), all of Klara's popularity transferred directly to Simone Green.

I had it! Popularity can be transferred. Proximity is key. All I had to do was get Simone's popularity to transfer to me.

I stayed where I was, observing Simone Green and her followers.

Simone Green, meet your new best friend.

# CHAPTER TEN

The Vote for Hank brainstorm wasn't impressive. It wasn't even a brainrain. More of a light drizzle. Actually, it was more like a few scattered, harmless clouds. Not even a cloud.

"Write it down," I said, holding my head.

"Hank," Frankie sighed, smushing his face. "For the last time, I'm not writing down 'Hank you very much'."

"How about 'Hank you mucho?' Has a bit more punch to it."

Frankie just breathed and looked at Ashley.

"We need to get something up there," I said. Frankie was up by an easel that we'd set up, but the thing was as clear and empty as a midsummer sky. "I thought there weren't any right answers in a brainstorm."

"You mean there aren't any *wrong* answers in a brainstorm," Ashley said. She was sprawled comfortably on the floor by the sofa, next to my feet. "But Zipzer-zee-doo-da is definitely wrong."

"What about, 'Vote Hank! It's as easy as an easel'?"

Frankie shook his head. "Now you're just looking around at things in the room. Think harder."

"Why does he get to hold the marker?" I asked Ashley. It was getting late, way past dinner, and we'd been going at it for hours, with nothing to show for it. "Maybe I should hold the marker for a while."

Ashley sort of grunted. Frankie put the marker in his pocket.

"We need to come up with something great," he said. "Something that grabs everyone's attention. Something that'll steal McKelty's thunder. Something that— Oh!"

"Don't mind me," my dad said. He had suddenly appeared behind the sofa, hovering. My dad likes to hover.

"Want to sit down, Mr Zipzer?" Ashley asked.

"No, no," he said. As usual, he just wanted to stand behind the sofa and listen – and freak everyone out by being there but not really being a part of things. Like a big doughy ghost that says a corny joke every now and then.

"Well, I'm off to bed for a good read," my mum said, coming in from the kitchen and holding a teen novel she's obsessed with. The one with all the vampires. "I'm almost finished."

Ashley raised herself slightly. "Have you got to the bit when hunky Lance sacrifices himself for love?"

"No, Ashley, I haven't."

"Oh. Sorry." Ashley lowered herself back down flat onto the carpet and started untying my shoelaces for no reason.

"'Night, kids," Mum said, sighing and leaving the vampire book behind. "Stan?" She motioned for Dad to follow.

"Be there in ten, love. Gotta hit the recycling first."

"Remember, you're not going to interfere."

"I'm going to recycle."

"Hey, I just found 50p!" Ashley said. "And a lollipop. There's good stuff under the sofa."

The door to Mum's room closed.

"Dad, we need help!" I whisper-shouted. "We've got nothing."

"We need some fresh ideas, Mr Zipzer," Frankie said. "The best we've got so far is getting Ashley's mum and dad to live-blog an operation where they sew 'Vote Hank' into one of their patients."

"It would get my vote," Ashley said and started in on the lollipop.

"Help me, Dad!"

He leaned over the sofa. "Mmm, I already promised your mum..."

"Come on, Dad. Come around to this side of the sofa and show us what you've got."

Dad leaned even further forward over me. At the very least, I wanted him to stop hovering. "Please, Dad. If you don't help then Nick McKelty is going to crush me. *His* dad's helping *him*."

Then, all at once, I no longer felt my dad's hovering presence. I heard him stomping away, mumbling, "That McKelty, I really don't like that McKelty..." He went to the hall cupboard, thumped around, and came out hoisting a giant cardboard box over his head, which he plopped down on the dinner table. And before I knew what was what, Dad had wheeled out a whiteboard, had set up his laptop and an extra computer, and had spread all the campaign stuff from his old crossword club days across the dinnertable.

"The key to a successful campaign," my dad said, "is grass-roots organization. Settle in, guys. We're gonna be here a while."

Ashley raised herself from the floor and climbed up to the sofa. Frankie handed over his marker.

McKelty was going down.

# CHAPTER ELEVEN

**From the electronic files of the Elect Emily Zipzer campaign:**

Campaign Log:

I spent the day observing Simone Green and her followers. I took a number of detailed photographs.

When I got home, I uploaded as many pictures of Westbrook Academy students as I could find, and cross-referenced all of these photos against those of Simone Green. I was looking for discrepancies.

I discovered some interesting results.

Simone Green's appearance is different from the rest of the general student body in three distinct ways:

1) She rolls up the sleeves of her school blazer exactly three times. Compared to others who do not roll up their sleeves even once, Simone Green's arms look well-ventilated and unrestrained.

2) Simone Green pops up her collar. Instead of folding her collar over her tie, she keeps it up. I believe she does this to make herself look taller, making sure her head is held high. As well, Simone's tie is tied very loosely around her neck.

3) Instead of black shoelaces, Simone Green wears bright pink shoelaces. Her laces are also much thicker than regular ones.

There are surely other ways that Simone Green sets herself apart from the rest of the student body, and thus maintains her popularity edge, but those three modifications to her uniform are a starting point in my Simone Green Strategy. I will make the same modifications. I will also go to school tomorrow wearing lipstick and a distinctly new hairstyle.

These modifications will buy me access into Simone Green's inner circle. Once I have infiltrated her circle, I will advance with all haste to Stage Two of the Strategy.

# CHAPTER TWELVE

The birds were singing again. My pillow
was moist with drool. I was so nice and
comfortable and warm. The warm, sleepy air
smelled like chocolate.

Then I opened my eyes.

"Hank!!!" It was my dad. His face was so
close that it didn't seem like a face at all.
More like a flesh bag with eyes and teeth,
and hot breath. "Wake up! Are you awake?"

"Where are Frankie and Ashley?" I
mumbled, and rolled over back into the
drool-soft cushion. I was on the sofa. What

was going on?

"Those wimps went home at midnight," he said and jostled my shoulder. "Well, what do you think?"

"Nine more minutes."

"What happened to not interfering?" I heard a voice ask — Mum.

"The boy was gonna lose to McKelty," Dad said. "Couldn't let that happen, could we, partner?"

He was talking to me. I rolled back over and got to a sitting position. I couldn't see anything; my eyes were still sleepy. There was something sticky in my hair. I scratched at it. Ashley's lollipop. It was stuck there pretty hard

Thankfully, my dad was no longer nose-to-nose with me. He was over by the kitchen with Mum, two hazy figures. "Sometimes there's a value to losing, especially if you lose for the right reason," Mum was saying.

"That's just something losers say to

make themselves feel better," my dad sniffed. "Ah! The cakes."

As I started to detach Ashley's lollipop from my hair, unsticking it hair by painful hair, I perked up. Why had I slept on the sofa? Why was my dad all hyped up and running around the place? Why was I looking at a life-size cardboard cutout of myself giving the thumbs-up? Was that me? Was I me? Or had I become someone else? (I was still pretty sleepy.)

I gave the lollipop a light yank and remembered a little more. I had asked my dad to help. And help he had.

The place was covered with campaign stuff. The life-size cutout was just the centrepiece. The dinner table was packed with fliers and badges, all neatly arranged in immaculate rows. A giant poster was displayed on the easel. It was good, too. It featured a picture of me tapping my noggin, above the words "THINK HANK" in all caps.

Not a bad campaign slogan.

Then things started getting hazy again.

No, wait, that was just smoke.

"What have you done?" Mum was yelling at Dad as he stood by the open oven, fanning smoke for dear life. "Why are you burning cakes?"

"For Hank to hand out. I was going to ice 'Vote Zipzer' on them, but then I had my great idea for a new slogan, 'Think Hank'. And then I remembered that I don't know how to ice."

Dad left the smoky oven for Mum to fan, and I think I fell asleep there for a moment, because next thing I knew, Dad was back at the sofa, his face again so close it no longer looked like a face. "Let's go get McKelty, yes?" he said and ripped the lollipop from my hair.

I screamed. I was much more awake now.

"Get a move on, councillor," he said. "We're leaving in five. We've got to pick up

some unburnt pastries from the deli. That's
OK, love, right?" he barked over to Mum.
Dad was really pretty hyped up.

But Mum was looking at the hallway,
where in my hazy, sleepy state I thought I
saw Simone Green.

"Oh, no," I blurted, and quickly ran my
fingers through my hair, brushed off my shirt
and put on a cool smile. I couldn't let her
see me like this!

But when I looked again, it was just Emily.

Except it wasn't really Emily. Her hair
was in, like, fifteen little braids, her tie was
untied, her collar turned up her sleeves
rolled up. Her pink shoelaces were fantastic.
Emily looked ... cool?

"Morning, Emily," Mum was saying. "What
are you ... I mean is that my lipstick..." Mum
turned back to the smoky stove, mumbling
to herself. "I mean, don't interefere. I'm not
interfering..."

Dad was busy mumbling to himself too,

something about how much he disliked
big Mr McKelty, and something about the
crossword club...

"Is it fancy dress day at school?" I asked
Emily.

"Hank!" Mum shouted from the kitchen.

"What?"

"Shhh."

"Everyone's awake, Mum! Why are you
shushing me—"

"Finito," Mum barked. "And why'd you let
your father get involved in your campaign?
You shouldn't let him mess about with this if
you don't want him to."

I started to open my mouth, but Dad's
voice seemed to be coming out of it.

"Remember, love, no interfering," he
said, tossing me my uniform, my book bag
and a little plastic bag with my toothbrush,
toothpaste and a packet of wet wipes.

"You interfered all last night!"

"I didn't interfere, I assisted," Dad said.

"The boy needed my help. He asked me of his own free will. And now you're interfering by not letting me ... interfere. See, it's one of those paradoxes, know what I mean? Hank, you can brush in the car." Having tossed aside the apron he had been wearing, Dad came zipping over, his face all greasy and his eyes wild and crazy. He zoomed right past Emily, then doubled back and did a kind of cartoon eyeball pop. "You look different. New glasses?"

"Stan!" Mum chucked the apron at him. Hard.

"What?"

"If you're going to interfere, interfere fairly. Ask Emily if she wants some cakes too."

"No, thank you," Emily said.

"Maybe next year," Dad said, and in a blur of action swept all the campaign materials into an extra-large duffel bag, tucked the life-size cardboard cutout of

Yours Truly under one arm, applied some of the sticky stuff from Ashley's lollipop to one of my campaign badges, and stuck it onto Emily's lapel. "Think Hank!" Then he was at the door. "Hank! Let's go beat McKelty. Show his dad a thing or two."

# CHAPTER THIRTEEN

I'm not one to tell on someone, especially if that someone happens to be my father. But Dad really should not have been driving in his state. When he wasn't raving about how much Mr McKelty bugged him and how we were going to win, he was nodding off at red lights, only waking up when I yelled at him to go. And since I was dog-tired from sleeping on the sofa, I wasn't a very reliable alarm clock for his red-light micro naps.

Miracle of miracles, we managed to get to Papa Pete's deli and parked safely –

more or less. Inside, Dad ran around to the back of the counter, and before Papa Pete could get two words in, my dad was stuffing Papa Pete's entire inventory of cannoli into the duffel bag containing my campaign stuff. "I'm requisitioning this material," he barked. "It's political. You know, for Hank's campaign."

"I didn't know you were running for office," Papa Pete said to me, remarkably unfazed by the robbery in progress.

"I guess so," I said, as Dad took one of the badges from the bag, slid it across the frosting on a cinnamon swirl, and stuck it to Papa Pete's shirtfront. "Think Hank," he said.

While Papa Pete was trying to figure out how he was going to serve his customers with no cannoli inventory, and why my dad was so hyped up, I asked Papa Pete if he could do me a strange favour. "Sure," he said, "of course, Hank."

"OK, this is going to sound weird, but..."

"I've heard it all before, my boy. So get it off your chest. Is it a girl?"

"Not really. Um, so if a guy named Mr Joy comes in and – actually, if anybody comes in – and they ask for something called gravlax—"

"What is a gravlax?"

"I'm not really sure," I said, "but I think it's food. Anyway, just say that you're all sold out. That your customers love gravlax, and that they can't get enough. Tell him to try again next week. Er, I'll explain it all later, promise."

"I don't understand what's happening this morning," Papa Pete said. "But anything you say, Hank, of course."

If there's one thing I love about Papa Pete, it's that he doesn't make me explain myself to him.

"And if big Mr McKelty comes in," my dad said, sweeping the last of the cannoli into the duffel, "give him this and tell him it's from big Mr Zipzer." He gave Papa Pete something from his pocket.

"You want me to give this big person a coupon for swimming lessons with Chet? What is the significance of—"

"No, no, no," Dad said, trying to reach across his body with his one semi-free arm into the other pocket. "This," he said, giving him a twenty-quid note.

"I'll keep this," Papa Pete said, and slipped it into his own pocket. "For all the inventory you, ah, *requisitioned*."

"No, I mean, urgh, that was my last twenty." Dad paused and ran his hand through his thinning hair. "Just tell him this, if big Mr McKelty comes in. Ask him: what's a seven-letter word for coward?"

"No," Papa Pete said. "I don't think I'll ask him this."

"But this is politics!" my dad cried.

"I don't like politics this early in the

morning."

After a pretty testy goodbye, Dad drove me the rest of the way to school.

I got out of the car, grabbed the duffel and the life-size cutout. I started to head inside, but my dad didn't pull away. Instead he put the handbrake on and closed his eyes.

"You all right?" I called through the window.

"Fine, fine," he mumbled. "Just gonna rest here a moment. Re-charge a bit."

"Dad, don't you have to go work or something?"

"Sure, sure, I'm on my way." His eyes were closed, and he was not in any way, shape or form about to drive off.

"Dad, really, this is embarrassing. Someone could recognize you."

But Dad had fallen into a deep coma.

I got out of there as fast as I possibly could. I put my head down and tried to make it for the entrance before anyone recognized me and figured out that I was related to the man who was sleeping in his car ... by the front of school.

Mr Joy saw me approach the school entrance. "Morning, Henry," he said. "Let me help you with that." Before I knew it, Mr Joy was carrying the life-size cutout for me. He looked it over enthusiastically. "You, sir, are a political animal. You're a shoo-in for the election, I just know it. Come Friday, you and I are going to stuff ourselves silly with gravlax. And if you need any gravlax before then, you know where to find me. I'll set you up. Just remember old Mr Joy when you become the prime minister someday."

We walked by the impossibly cool Simone Green in the corridor. She stopped to watch us pass, judging us the whole time. She regarded me with a brutal eye-roll death ray, and a weird and devastating noise that sounded like "khhhhh".

"I really think you'll love what Chef

Anton came up with for today's lunch," Mr Joy was saying, oblivious to how brutally Simone Green had just destroyed me. "Today he has made bone-marrow pancakes with a jicama reduction..."

# CHAPTER FOURTEEN

Frankie and Ashley were waiting for me at my locker. And I didn't arrive alone. Thanks to my life-size cutout, I had a group of kids following me.

"That's so awesome!" Frankie cried.

"You're going to win for sure," Ashley said.

"Like you guys said, we had to do something to steal momentum from McKelty." I stood the cutout next to my locker. Kids passing by gave it the thumbs-up. "This cutout here," I paused to caress its arm, "isn't quite as cool as the golf cart, but it will do the trick."

"I thought you knew?" Ashley said. "Mr Rock confiscated the golf cart yesterday."

I gave the cutout a high five. "I think I'm getting my mojo back."

"I think we're going to run away with this thing," Frankie said.

"You guys ain't seen nothin' yet." I opened my duffel of campaign stuff. Some of it was smeared with cannoli cream, but the cream was delicious and the rest of the materials were clean ... ish. "And check out the poster."

"'Think Hank!'" Ashley cried. "That's great. Much better than—"

"Hank you mucho," I said.

Another kid came and high-fived my cutout a five. "Let's go and hang up the poster and set up the booth before first lesson."

We ran through the corridors to the

bulletin board where we were allowed to place our posters. Everyone cleared a path for us and stood in awe as went about our official political business. Nothing says official political business like a life-size cardboard cutout.

Emily and McKelty had both already hung up their posters. McKelty's was slick, well-made and bossy. It had a picture of him with the slogan: "Vote McKelty. Because only the best can give YOU the best."

Emily's was, uh ... different. It didn't have a picture of her or anything, just this weird abstract shape, with some ovals and a curly line. Under the weird shape, it said: "Emilé".

We hung up my poster, and it looked great. The picture of me was strong and confident, yet simple and human. And the look in my eyes seemed to give you the impression that a vote for me was like a vote for destiny, that I was going to lead this school into a fantastic new age!

My voters loved it too. "Yours is the best by far," Cordy Blackwell said as she passed by. "Great picture."

In the common room, Frankie and Ashley and I set up our stall, which was really just a table with a thousand cannoli on it, watched over by my cardboard likeness.

And what a likeness!

Everything was going great! Even Simone Green and some of her clique of followers seemed to approve. No one can resist the all-powerful draw of cannoli – not even Simone Green.

# CHAPTER FIFTEEN

**From the electronic files of the Elect Emily Zipzer campaign:**

Campaign log:

Today at 7.52 a.m. I made my first attempt to infiltrate Simone Green's clique. I watched them on the playground for several minutes before approaching. They were not playing sports, nor reading or double-checking their homework, nor engaging in intellectual discussions. Instead they were sitting on benches and gossiping about some boy, or boys, that they "like, totes like". I can't be certain. Their vocal patterns are difficult to parse.

Transforming myself physically had been a chore. I spent three hours last night braiding my hair into 18 tight little knots. And I got up at five this morning so I could get dressed and then spent the next hour meticulously deconstructing and modifying various attributes of my school uniform, all to give the impression that I couldn't be bothered to put on my uniform properly. Then, after making myself look slovenly, I spent another hour meticulously applying layers of make-up.

I watched and listened to the girls blabber about boys, inching my way closer and closer, until I hovered on the outer edge of their circle. I chose to make my entry into their group at 7.53 for a reason: as class starts at 8.00, I felt five minutes on interaction was a nice, short window –

not enough time for me to err disastrously. Not enough time for me to stand out as an interloper, a poser.

Simone was saying, "But then I'm thinking, 'Do I really like Kieron, 'cos his dancing is lame.'"

Adelle, her main follower, replied: "Yeah, that boy's a fool, you know."

Simone: "But then I'm thinking, I don't like any boy in that band. Once or More is done. They're over!"

Me: "Finito."

I'm not sure why I said "finito". I believe I've heard Mum say it on occasion. In any event, the girls all looked my way. They regarded me silently, as if trying to decide whether my comment was relevant. But then they continued on in a similar vein as before.

Simone: "So anyway, I bought this right nice top the other day..."

At that moment, they began heading for class. I trailed after them in the outer circle.

Adelle, Simone's chief follower, came up next to me. "Finito? Who's finito?"

I believe I said something along the lines of, "They're like, you know, whatevs, don't be jelly..." and trailed off. Adelle quickly pushed ahead to her usual place by Simone's side.

Adelle, Simone and the rest of the crew were not overly impressed with my first interaction. But all the same I considered this encounter a success. No one wondered for long why I was there, no one seemed to recognize me from class, and no one asked me to leave.

So I didn't.

# CHAPTER SIXTEEN

All day long I was in the zone. I had my
mojo working. Every little I thing I did was
right on the money. I could do no wrong.
Even when I did do something wrong, it
was right, oh so right. It's like every single
hole I dug was turning up nothing but gold.
Beautiful, lovely, clinking gold bullion. I
was swimming in pieces o' eight. I was the
captain. I was heading for world presidency,
world domination, a Hankification of this
Westbrook nation.

The first piece of golden luck came

during my geography lesson. We were studying soil erosion. Pretty boring stuff, so I excused myself from class for a quick "campaign stop" at the loo. But I got distracted and decided to head over to the corridor with the posters to check on my likeness.

Someone was standing in front of my poster, blocking it with his body, like he was in the act of defacing my face and trying not to get caught. This someone had perfectly combed blond hair.

McKelty turned to me. He'd drawn a handlebar moustache on my beautiful face.

"Something of an improvement, don't you think, Hank?" He sauntered off, grinning his evil grin.

I didn't know what to do. By "Nutrition by Chef Anton" everyone would see my ruined poster, and by lunchtime I'd be known throughout Westbrook as Handlebar Hank. I was ruined. McKelty had hit me hard, right where it hurts: my gorgeous face.

Back in class, I returned to my desk. We had to make diagrams of different soil layers with big, black Sharpie markers. I was miserable. My perfect poster was defaced. And every time I looked up, I'd see McKelty smirking at me.

I tried to focus on my geography worksheet, but it was hopelessly boring. Even my geography partner, Jennifer Granneli, was just drawing little Sharpie freckles on her arm to pass the time. "I've always wanted freckles," she said. "And now I've got them. And now you do too," she said, and dotted my arm with a giggle.

That's when my great idea hit me.

"Freckles are great," I said. "But you know what my dream is?"

"What?"

"A moustache. A big thick, handlebar."

"You should follow your dreams," she said.

So while the rest of the class was drawing subsoil, I drew a perfect handlebar moustache onto my upper lip

"Wow, it looks awesome!" Jennifer said.

"Really? I knew it would."

"Here, look," she handed me a pocket mirror. And let me tell you something: my moustache looked unbelievable. I planned to grow a nice thick one as soon as I was able.

Then I wiggled my upper lip at Jennifer. She got the giggles. Frankie was at the next desk heard the commotion, and looked over. I puffed out my lip, and wiggled my 'tache at him with wide, googly eyes. He got the giggles so badly he looked like he was about to explode. He had to stuff his head in a cupboard below the desks to let it out. Word got around class about my moustache, that I'd wiggle it at anyone who looked at me. So whenever Miss Adolf was preoccupied, one kid or another would look at me, I'd wiggle my 'tache and bulge out my eyes, and in no time everyone had the giggles. The best kind of giggles too, when it's inappropriate to laugh but you want to so hard it actually hurts your lungs.

But I got careless. I just kept looking around for anyone to wiggle my 'tache at, and I was going rapid fire around the room, until my eyes landed on a certain teacher of mine with no sense of humour.

"HENRY ZIPZER!"

The class erupted. Eighteen kids let out all their pent up giggles in one snorty, giggly explosion. Miss Adolf's eyes were bulged out too, but not in a giggly way. All the muscles in her neck were popping out as she raised her sword and slashed it at the door.

"GO TO THE WC THIS INSTANT AND WASH THAT THING FROM YOUR FACE! NOW, NOW, NOW! I DON'T CARE IF YOU HAVE TO SCRUB AWAY YOUR ENTIRE UPPER LIP, DO NOT RETURN WITH ANY TRACE OF THAT THING. DO YOU UNDERSTAND?"

I wiggled my 'tache one last time as I bolted for the door, and just before getting out I threw up my arms, and yelled, "Hank for President!"

I could hear the class cheering two corridors down.

As I made my way to the loo, I stopped at each class's door, looked in the little window, and wiggled my 'tache until everyone was in stitches.

Within two minutes, Jennifer Granneli came marching down the hall, sporting her very own handlebar. She high-fived me with a loud slap "Hank for President!"

In no time, kids were bursting through doors all sporting handlebars. I had started a handlebar revolution. Everyone was laughing and yelling "Hank for President" in the hallways, yelling so loud I had no doubt in my mind that McKelty heard it all, and that he was probably crying.

# CHAPTER SEVENTEEN

Before it was even "Nutrition by Chef Anton" time, my new slogan of "Follow your dreams: grow a handlebar" had become something of an underground calling card. If I had to guess, I'd say that one out of four kids in Westbrook had drawn a handlebar on their lips; everyone else didn't have the guts to get in trouble.

All the moustaches had to be washed off, of course. But the cool thing was to not wash it off *all the way.*

McKelty stood behind his booth in the

common room, with his hands pressed flat on the table, so his shoulders were raised up and he looked angry. "Vote McKelty. Vote McKelty. Only the best can get YOU the best. Vote McKelty on Thursday."

But the way he was saying his slogans was really off-putting. It was like he was yelling at everyone, the way your father might yell at you for breaking a lamp or something, after Dad's had a long, frustrating day. Not a single soul was at McKelty's booth. And anyone who walked past started to run nervously as soon as McKelty started hollering his campaign slogans. He made one little girl freeze up and cry. She just stood there, crying, while McKelty kept hollering, until I went over and brought her to my booth.

"There, there," I said, putting my arm around her shoulder. "Let's keep you away from that mean, bad boy. Would a little dessert make you feel better?"

"Uh-huh," she whimpered.

"Hey, Zipperbutt!" McKelty bellowed. "That's my voter! You're stealing my vote. Hey, little girl, what's my name again?"

"McStinky!" she shouted.

"Things are going to change around here when I get power!" McKelty shouted back. Then he remembered himself and added, "Because only the best can give YOU the best."

"Don't worry about McStinky," I said to the little girl. "He didn't take his antibiotics."

I brought her over to my booth's abundant spread of Councillor Hank Cannoli. We had a swarm of people clamouring for them. Frankie and Ashley had to scramble to hand them out fast enough. But if you approached with a moustache, or pretended to draw a handlebar across your lips, you got two.

"Remember to vote!" I cried. "And remember, there's plenty more where these came from. Make me your councillor, and we'll stuff ourselves silly with pastries!"

Everyone cheered.

Frankie handed me a megaphone. I turned it up full blast and pointed it at the scowling McKelty. "What's my name again?!"

"HANK!" The crowd answered in chorus.

"That's right," I said, "HANK FOR STUDENT COUNCIL! GROW A HANDLEBAR!"

McKelty's cheek twitched.

I gave the megaphone back to Frankie.

"McKelty's finished," I said to my staff. "He's toast by Chef Anton, covered with bone marrow and farfalle balls."

"Don't count him out yet," Ashley said. "He looks like he's plotting something."

I glanced across the room. McKelty was in the same sulking position. Not moving, with his face tensed up. "Nah, it just looks like he's got stomach issues. He must have had some gravlax."

# CHAPTER EIGHTEEN

We had to take a pause from the election in order to go to class, but lunchtime came around quickly. The minute the class was let out we went back to the common room, where two kids with faded moustaches from the year above us were posing for a picture by my cardboard cutout.

"Is this OK, Councillor Hank?" they asked.

"Of course," I said. "I encourage it."

One candidate whose presence was there, but who was not there in person, was "Emilé". She had finally set up her booth.

There were no badges or fliers or campaign pamphlets. Instead, the whole booth was covered with old looking posters of random things: heavily made-up eyes, a cactus, a rabbit perched on a rocking chair, city lights in a puddle, a flower growing out of a seashell. And underneath all those random images were single words printed in bold black letters, all lowercase, that said things like: "image?", "fashion?", "bliss?", "time?", "accessorize?" and "whatevs!". In the centre of all that was that same abstract logo or insignia or design from her poster.

"What the...?"

"I'm not sure what Emily is going for," Ashley said.

"I don't think she knows, either," Frankie said.

"Ah, there you are!" Mr Joy was at the doorway, holding yet another white take-away box. "I didn't see you in the cafeteria, and I thought you might be a little peckish.

I know you're putting in the hours trying to wrap this election up, and I admire that."

"Thanks, Mr Joy," I said. I could smell what was inside that box. I could smell it even before he walked into the room.

"It's yesterday's," he said, "but the cafeteria staff assured me that they've kept our favourite treat nice and cool."

A few kids started to trickle outside from the cafeteria. Mr Joy saw all the cannoli spread across the table, and smiled, shaking his head. "You really are a natural-born politician," he said, with a knowing wink. "You're not trying to bribe your way to election victory, are you?"

"Bribe? Why Mr Joy, that's a dirty word," I said right back at him, tapping the white take-away box. I picked up a piece of cannoli and passed it his way. "Care for a little treat?"

"Why not?" he said, taking the offering. "I think we're going to get along nicely, Mr

Zipzer." He made the sign of the handlebar, then raised the cannoli to his mouth, smacking his lips. I kept a big politician's smile plastered on my face.

He popped the cannoli in. I winced at hearing his teacher-chewing noises. His eyes rolled back in his head in sweet delight. But then, all at once, his eyes bulged out. He grabbed his throat. He opened his mouth wide. I saw every last bit of undigested foodstuff in his mouth. I saw the fillings in his back molars. I saw his tonsils.

"EEEEEEEEE!!!!!" Mr Joy screamed, jumping and shaking his hands in the classic freak-out gesture. "SO MUCH CHILLI!!! EEEEEEEEEEE!!!!! WATER!!! FIRE EXTINGUISHER!!! EEEEE!!!!"

Then Mr Joy could only make this cat-coughing-up-a-hairball sound as he ran wild around the common room. Frankie, Ashley and I all gaped at each other in confusion.

But behind Frankie's left earlobe, I saw

something lurking in the shadows. A shock of blond hair.

"McKelty's behind this," I whispered to my mates. "He'll do anything to win!"

Frankie dived for the wastebasket. He found an economy size bottle of Crazy Cordwainer's Doom Sauce and held it up: empty. In the shadows, the shock of blond hair was shaking with laughter. McKelty stepped into the light and stood in his booth, watching me with a self-satisfied smirk.

But a slow smile spread across my face. "I'm sorry, Mr Joy," I said, looking McKelty dead in the eye, "but you have failed the 'Zipzer Hot Cannoli Challenge'. Who will be the first to conquer the Italian inferno?"

All the kids who had wandered in from the cafeteria rushed to the booth. Everyone was eager to take the inferno challenge, scream and run around the room holding their throats and gasping like they were astronauts in space without their helmets.

Even Mr Joy came back for another try. "Outrageous! Unbelievable! I love it, Mr Zipzer! You really are a prince among men! How about you give old Mr Joy another go?"

"Certainly!"

He took a bite, grabbed his throat and started going nuts, running around the room screaming and laughing with everyone else. Everyone except McKelty. He hadn't budged from his hulking position.

As the crowd dwindled and the last few stragglers were in the tail-end of their inferno freak-outs, I took a seat and helped myself to a snack. I was really hungry.

"Nice one, Hank," Frankie said, as we sat back and savoured my inevitable victory. "Nail that speech tomorrow and the election's all yours."

"Oh yeah, the speech," I said. Then it all clicked. "The speech? The speech! Oh no, the speech!"

"Don't tell me you haven't started it yet," Ashley said.

I was about to take another bite of my snack when it dawned on me that for the past few minutes I'd been absentmindedly snacking on the gravlax! And it wasn't agreeing with my stomach, not one bit. A sharp shooting pain sliced across my gut. My body was telling me that it wanted that gravlax out of there, pronto!

"I'll see you guys later!" I said, walking as serenely as I could for the hallway, so McKelty wouldn't see my pain. "I need to make a campaign stop, of the sitting variety. Ohhhhhh..."

As soon as I hit the hallway, I made a desperate dash to my political headquarters: the WC.

# CHAPTER NINETEEN

My stomach doom had returned with a
vengeance. No matter what I did during the
rest of the school day, I remembered that
I had to write a speech that evening, and
even though it was Wednesday, it felt like
Sunday/Monday in my gut.

I wondered: *Is this what it would feel
like all the time if I got elected?* I had all
these people trying to take me down, all
these people telling me what to do, and a
headmaster who wouldn't let me go half a
day without trying to force-feed me gravlax.

None of those things would go away if I got on the school council. They'd probably just get worse.

And I still had that speech to write. A wad of partially digested gravlax swam up into my throat.

After the final bell rang, I wandered around the school trying to find Mr Rock.

He was in the assembly hall, next to McKelty's confiscated golf cart. Mr Rock was pounding at some part of the engine with a hammer.

"Oh, hi, Hank," he said when he noticed me. He gave the engine another whack. "Between you and me, this cart hates wheelies."

"Is that why you're hitting it?"

"I'm trying, Hank, to repair it," he said, and smacked it again. "I don't know *how* to repair it – I don't know the first thing about golf carts – but I think it's always a good idea to try something new once a day."

My stomach gurgled. "Oooh."

"You all right, Hank?"

"Yeah... No, not really," I said sitting down, hunched over. "It's just too much gravlax ... and this election ... and this speech tomorrow..."

"And let me guess," Mr Rock said, "you haven't started it."

"Uh-huh."

"That sounds so unlike you."

That put a smile on my face. If only Mr Rock could be my regular teacher!

"Let me ask you a question, and then we'll get back to smashing golf carts," Mr Rock said. "Why do you want to win this election?"

"That's easy. To beat McKelty."

"And why do you want to be on school council?"

That was a good question ... and a second question, which wasn't part of the deal. "Can we do some smashing now? Or how about video games? Have you ever played Digging for Gold? You just cruise around the beach digging holes. But there's gold in some of them holes..." I trailed off when I heard how idiotic I sounded. But the sad part was, when he asked me about being on the council, all I could imagine was playing Digging for Gold all Saturday long.

"Let me put the question another way," Mr Rock said. "Why do you like to play Digging for Gold?"

"That's easy, too! To get gold. And if you get enough gold, you can upgrade your shovel to—"

"Let me guess: dig more holes."

"You got it!"

"So you must really like digging holes?"

I thought I knew the answer to this one too, but the way Mr Rock was smiling at me made think again. "I guess I do like digging holes. It's relaxing. The sky in the video game is so blue, and the clouds are so fluffy and white, and it's satisfying to dig a bunch of holes."

"Ah, this sounds like when I was in my band, Tripod Vision," Mr Rock said. "I thought being in a band meant making great music that changed people's lives."

"What was it really about?"

"Hanging out at parties." Mr Rock smiled with a faraway look, but I couldn't pick up on what he was thinking.

He snapped out of it. "Hank, it's important that you know whether you really want to do this."

"But how do I know?"

He shrugged. "I don't know. But once you know what you want, you can really be yourself. And when that happens, life is one giant golf cart that you get to smash."

"You mean repair."

"Sure." He held out the hammer. "Want to see if you can repair this golf cart?"

"Do I ever!"

# CHAPTER TWENTY

**From the electronic files of the Elect Emily Zipzer Campaign:**

Campaign log:

All day long I shadowed Simone Green and her followers. After the "finito incident" before school, I decided that I should stay quiet and observe until I gained a greater understanding of their speech patterns.

This was not a difficult task. Quickly I developed an ear for their slang, and with that I was able to penetrate their thoughts.

Their thoughts were simple and largely revolved around things like their love of cheesy chips, their disdain for some sort of performer named Blane who had publicly betrayed Kaitlin, so he could go with Jezebel on a steamy vacation to Fiji. But Kaitlin was like "nuh-uh" and … you get the idea.

Simone had plenty of thoughts about Westbrook Academy, which she gave voice to constantly. School was "boring" and "lame", especially biology, which was "double boring". And it was "really stupid" that the school had no magazines or TVs to look at, and a "crime" that Westbrook didn't offer a class on "shopping".

While everyone was waiting for our history lesson to begin, I felt confident enough about my research that I decided to initiate Stage Two of my Simone Strategy. I went to the back, where Simone and crew were gossiping about Blane, told them that I was running for student council, which was totally lame, but like, I figured I could do some cool stuff, if I could even be bothered. Simone asked what kind of cool stuff. I told her that there should be more cheesy chips, all the time, and a double shopping class, instead of boring biology.

Simone told her Number Two, Adelle, to move, and asked me to sit next to her. Success! I was in her popularity bubble, and it felt totally amazing! And then Simone even asked me if she could come over tonight so she could tell me more things I should do so that school isn't so horrible all the time. And she asked loudly too, so everyone knew that she and I had plans tonight.

But my room was a dorky disaster. Running home and working fast, I hid all my boring biology textbooks, put up three posters of Hunky Blane over my bed and exchanged all the solemn and serious black pens on my desk for girly glitter gel colours.

Simone just loved my room. She told

me all sorts of totes wicked ideas to improve the school. She shared with me that pink shoelaces were out, and that she was thinking about switching to yellow. We slagged off Hunky Blane, we talked about how hard it was to be Kaitlin right now, what with Blane and Jezebel on their steamy holiday in Fiji, but that Kaitlin needed to get herself together and just release her new video already ... Simone and I were bonding.

And then crash went my house of cards.

"Ew, what's that?"

She had spotted my sweet lizard Katherine, sitting on my pillow below the poster of Blane where he's wearing a tank top.

"Is that, like, your lizard? It's looking at me."

But Simone was mistaken; Katherine was looking at me, staring into my soul.

I hedged, I stammered, I mumbled something about how it was our neighbour's gross lizard, and it was always coming in here and getting its gross claws all over my stuff. But I couldn't continue. Katherine was looking at me, the real me, and I was breaking her heart.

"I can't do this any more!" I blurted. "I find school stimulating and enthralling, I find cheesy chips repulsive and loaded with saturated fats, and I love that lizard with all my heart! She is mine, and I am hers!"

I was all set to be banished from Simone's realm with an eye-roll ... but it didn't come.

"That's cool," she said. "I like lizards too. It's really cool that you're hanging out with us girls now."

I was dumbfounded. Later, after she had left, I wondered: could I become popular just being myself?

Then I suddenly had a disturbing thought: popularity can be transferred through proximity, but maybe it was just as possible that dorkiness could be transferred too?

# CHAPTER TWENTY-ONE

I don't mind public speaking. I'm actually
pretty good at it. The problem is that I'm
only good when I'm improvising, Zipzer
style. If I have to write the speech and read
it in front of people – nuclear disaster!

"Can't I just wing it?" I asked Frankie and
Ashley. They were helping me get ready
for the big speech in my room. "It would be
more me if I just make it up as I go. More
authentic."

"I think it's better to have something on
paper," Frankie said. "You could forget one

of your main points if you're improvising."

"But I don't have any main points!" I waved my speech at him. "Hello! I'm holding a blank sheet of paper."

"That's why we're writing a speech," Ashley said.

"I'll just go by feelings, you know," I said. "It'll be great."

"It *could* be great," Ashley said, taking the blank paper from me and then sitting at my desk chair. "Or you might get up there and have zero ideas. In front of the whole school. That would be the opposite of great."

"You know what would be the opposite of great?" I asked. "If I have to read a speech in front of the whole school." I flopped down face-first onto my bed and buried my head in the pillow. "I think I have to drop out of the race."

"What?" Frankie said, and began pacing my room. "Drop out? No one's dropping out!

If you do, McKelty will rule Westbrook with an iron fist."

Ashley came and sat by my bed. "It's OK, Hank," she said. "We'll make visual cue cards. You won't have to read. We'll draw little pictures on pieces of paper to remind you of what to talk about, and you can just wing it from there. Frankie will hold them up for you. And I'll draw the little pictures."

"Why do you get to draw them?" Frankie asked.

"'Cos it was my idea," Ashley said.

"But I'm great at drawing! You guys are making a huge mistake."

"Ashley's drawing them," I said decisively, sitting up. I was feeling a little better. But Frankie was about one step from walking out on my campaign.

"Great," Ashley said. "This is good." She sat up and reached for the biggest book on my nightstand – Ninja Secrets – to use for a hard surface. "So, Hank. Let's hear them.

Tell me your great ideas and I'll sketch them out."

I looked at Ashley. I looked at the blank paper, her pen ready and waiting for input.

"What if I don't have any great ideas?" I asked, wanting nothing more than to bury my head in the pillow again.

"We'll start with some good ideas and make them better," Ashley said. "See, aren't you glad you're not winging it? This could be you tomorrow. So, let's do it now. Come on, shoot. Let's hear those ideas."

The only idea I had in my head was that my stomach was killing me. But I was pretty sure that wasn't a good idea. It wasn't even an idea. More like a premonition, a taste of things to come.

"Come on, Hank," Frankie said. "Just say what you want to do when you're on the school council."

"That's the problem, guys. I don't have a clue." My head was steadily inching downwards for a pillow face-plant.

"What about getting rid of the new cafeteria menu?" Frankie said. "That'd be great. Mention that, the simple-lunches strategy."

"There's no way I could do that," I said. "Mr Joy loves Chef Anton's menu."

"Oh, that doesn't matter," Frankie said, pacing with his hands behind his back. He was getting amped up. "Kids will vote for you if you say you'll try to go back to the old menu. Draw that one, Ashley. That Hank will get rid of the new cafeteria menu."

Ashley's pen tapped the paper. "Um... I'm not really sure how to draw that..."

"It's easy!" Frankie almost shouted. "You just draw one of those new meals and put an X through it, and then you—"

"Those meals are complicated," Ashley said. "I don't think I can draw them."

"Look. Lemme see that." Frankie snatched the pen and paper from Ashley and started sketching.

"What's that?" she asked.

"Open your eyes, Ash," Frankie said.
"That's a farfalle ball."

I tuned them out. This just wasn't
working. I didn't know why I wanted to be
school councillor.

As quiet as could be, I slipped out of my
room. With my friends arguing over farfalle
balls, they didn't notice.

# CHAPTER TWENTY-TWO

I was really low. My stomach was ruined.
And I had so little energy that all I could
do was just sort of wander around the
darkened living room, looking at lamps and
tracing wood grain patterns with my finger.

"What are you doing?" a girl's voice
asked out of nowhere.

"Huh?" I spun around. At first I thought
I was looking at the person – or concept –
that is Emilé, since she was holding a book.
But then she stepped out of the shadowy
hallway. "Oh my golf cart," I sputtered.

"You're Simone Green!"

"I know you," she said. "You're that president guy, or something."

"Yup, that's me," I said nonchalantly. "Just preparing for tomorrow's election ... or something." I sat down at the dining table, where a lot of Dad's campaign stuff was spread out. I started rifling through some of the papers and pretended to be very busy reading them in near total darkness. "It's not a big deal. But what are you doing here?"

"Having a hang." She shrugged. "Well, see ya, I guess."

She walked past me with the book, her arms covering the cover, but I recognized it right away. The book had lived on Emily's nightstand since she was three. It was called *Everything You Ever Wanted to Know About Lizards.*

Just as I was thinking that maybe Simone Green wasn't that cool and intimidating, she called back to me, "G'luck on the speech tomorrow, Harvey."

The speech. The speech! The stupid speech! I didn't have a clue what I wanted to say. I didn't have a clue what I wanted to do on school council. Come on, Harvey. Think! Harvey had nothing. But I could hear Hank loud and clear. What Hank wanted to do was withdraw from the election.

But I couldn't. Frankie and Ashley were counting on me. My moustache army were ready to launch a revolution with their votes. My dad had nearly lost his sanity trying to help. I mean, the dining table was *still* covered with all the fliers and badges and posters he'd made, and this was just the stuff we couldn't fit in the bag. I couldn't resign. I had to go through with it.

I just needed an idea. One good idea that I could tell the school, which would fire me up again for the final push. Just one thing I could say that really felt like me. So I

looked through Dad's box of old campaign
papers. Maybe he'd already come up with
that idea?

I dug through the box, and at the very
bottom was an old crossword puzzle.
Crosswords are how my dad procrastinates;
they're his version of Digging for Gold.
But there was something weird about this
crossword puzzle. It was blank, unfinished.
I've never seen any of Dad's crosswords in
a state other than finished, leaving not one
square blank, and the amount of time it
took my dad to finish it triumphantly noted
at the top.

In this crossword, only one square was
filled in, the one in the very top left. It
was the letter "Z", followed by five blank
spaces. The clue for 1 across was: cowardly,
synonym. Next to the clue was a small
smudged circle in the paper. It looked like
a single teardrop that had dried. I knew the
answer: Zipzer. Underneath the grid, it read,

"Puzzle by B. McKelty".

"So now you know the real story," another voice from the hallway said. It was my dad, in his tattered old bathrobe. "I never ran for secretary of my crossword club, Hank." He took the old crossword puzzle and shook his head. "I'd wanted to. I didn't like the way Big McKelty was running things. He was spending our budget on luncheons and pricey V-neck sweaters so he could look more 'secretarial'. But it was supposed to be about the crosswords, you know? So all year long I talked a big game about running, about how things would be different when I was secretary. But when the day came to sign up for the elections, I pretended I was sick. I couldn't stand the thought of losing to him. So you see, Hank, you've already got more courage than your old man."

"Thanks, Dad."

"I want you to have something." He took

out a pen from his bathrobe and slid it across the table. "It's my lucky pen. I used this bad boy the first time I—"

"Completed a crossword?"

"Fished my lucky pants out from behind the radiator. I was afraid to do it, because that radiator was hot, and I don't like getting burned. But this pen was the perfect size for the job. So don't chew the end of it, OK?"

"I definitely won't."

# CHAPTER TWENTY-THREE

After that little heart-to-heart with Dad, I
went back to my room and, together with
my staff, hacked out something of a speech.
We were going to hit all the fan favourites:
double lunch periods, shorter school days,
no-homework weekends – stuff that I'd love
to see happen one day.

Next morning, after heading to my
"political headquarters" for a brief campaign
stop of the sitting variety, I met up with
my mates at 7.45 a.m. They were already
waiting for me in a little room outside

the assembly hall, where they store AV equipment and – if you believe the rumour – the school caretaker's severed finger. Emilé was already in there too, practising her own speech. It seemed to be entirely comprised of hair tosses, and lots of sounds like *tahhhh* and *ugghhh*.

Ashley and Frankie started going through the cue cards with me. I knew my material cold.

"You got this," Frankie said, after I'd delivered a thoroughly convincing argument for no-homework weekends. "But one thing is bothering me: where's McKelty?"

"Yeah, where is he?" I asked. "Emilé, did your political-science forecasting predict that McKelty would drop out? Or could he be planning some sort of surprise? What does your data make of this?"

Emilé shrugged, the exact same way Simone Green shrugs at everything. But then, for only a moment, she dropped the cool act and winked at me with a knowing smile.

I grimaced and pulled my troops aside. "Oh no," I whispered.

"What?" Ashley whispered back.

"I think Emily is about to steal this election. She's been playing me since the beginning. She's set up everything. She's had me chasing McKelty, so that I'd take him out."

"So?" Ashley and Frankie said.

"I didn't take her seriously. I was so focused on beating McKelty that I played right into her hands. But I think Emily might be some sort of political mastermind. 'Emilé' was just a ruse to make us think she had no chance! I think I've been sabotaged!"

Ashley shook her head. "No, McKelty's probably just running late... Or maybe he's planning something really cool."

"Like riding onto stage on a Hoverboard," Frankie added. "We should have thought of that!"

My heart was beating. I started sweating. I found it nearly impossible to swallow. "Guys, I can't feel my hands. And my stomach—"

Just then, the door swung open. My team and I held our breath, ready for McKelty to swoop in on a Hoverboard, or maybe even a jet pack.

But it was just Mr Joy. "OK everyone," he announced. "You guys go on in five. Let's keep it clean and civil. I expect you to conduct yourselves in a manner befitting Westbrook Academy. May the best man win."

"Humanoid," my little sister Emily said, dropping her Simone Green act. "Humanoid more accurately reflects the range of candidates, Mr Joy."

"Works for me," said Mr Joy. He looked around, and checked his clipboard. "And where's the other one, McBlondie, or whatever the *humanoid's* name is."

"He doesn't appear to be within the walls

of this small room," my sister said.

"That's a shame," Mr Joy said, although he looked pleased. "Er, Henry, a moment alone, if you don't mind?"

He motioned me over to a corner with AV cables. "I stopped by the Spicy Salami on my way here," he whispered.

"Really?"

"Yes, I wanted to pick up some of your grandfather's famous gravlax for this special occasion. Unfortunately, he said he'd just sold out. I didn't see how it was possible to sell out of a lunch dish by 7.45 a.m., but—"

"I told you it was really popular," I said.

"Indeed," he said and reached into his bag, pulling out another white take-away box. "So I asked the cafeteria staff to find you some of theirs."

He handed the box to me. It definitely smelled fishy.

"Is this next Tuesday's gravlax?" I asked.

"Oh no," he said. "It's from this week's batch. But not to worry: I've been told that gravlax stays fresh for up to three days. Go ahead and dig in. I know you want to."

I opened it up and took the smallest bite possible.

"Dig in, Henry, you deserve it. Now, I'll go and warm up the crowd for you. I'd wish you luck, but you don't need it."

He left the room. A nano-second later, I spat a mouthful of old salmon mush onto an overhead projector. But it was too late. My body had already absorbed too many gravlax juices, and my stomach was doing a gymnastic floor routine worthy of Olympic gold. Through a crack in the door I heard the crowds mumbling and talking, a nervous white noise echoing off the high ceilings.

Why wasn't McKelty here yet? What was my sister planning? Why did it feel like there were thumb tacks sloshing around in my digestive tract? I heard all those kids out there in the assembly hall.

"What did Mr Joy want?" Frankie asked.

"Just to poison me with more gravlax," I said. "And to wish me luck."

"You don't need luck, buddy," Frankie said. "You got this."

Suddenly I felt like I was missing something. I patted my pockets for Dad's lucky pen. "My dad's lucky pen! I must have dropped it."

I started for the door, but my staff blocked my way. "There's no time," Ashley said.

"But I need that pen!" I yelled, and then was nearly floored by a wave of pain in my guts. The gravlax! "I need to make one last 'campaign stop'. Ohhhh..."

# CHAPTER TWENTY-FOUR

Dad's lucky pen was right where I thought
it would be, in my lucky loo stall, where
I'd made all my "campaign stops" since I
first tasted the gravlax. As I was washing
my hands, I thought I heard quiet weeping
coming from one of the other stalls.

And then someone was talking through
the tears.

"Dad, I know I've let the family down, but
there's no way I can win the election now.
I'm so sorry. Hello? Dad? Are you there?"

Then the stall opened. It was Nick

McKelty. He jumped when he saw me and quickly wiped away his tears.

"Happy now?" he said, scowling at his own reflection in the mirror.

"Happier than you" is what I wanted to say ... but I didn't. I saw my arm moving towards his body, and though I tried to stop it, I could only look on as I patted his shoulder. "It's only the school council. Who cares?"

"You've got no idea what it's like to have a father who puts so much pressure on you to succeed."

"My dad really wants me to win this, too," I said.

"No, you don't understand," he said. "Your dad doesn't know anything about winning. My dad is a winner, and I wanted to win this election to show him that I could win, too. To be like him. So he might, you know, notice me."

It took me a second to work out my

feelings after that one. McKelty had just insulted my dad. But at the same time, he was a mess, and it seemed like his family was an even bigger mess.

I tried to stop what I did next from happening. It was like one of those dreams when you wake up and know you're going to kick your leg, or scream, but can't do anything about it. So before I knew what was really going on, I had wrapped my arms around that sad sack with blond hair, and we hugged it out big-time.

"I'm so sorry, Nick. I didn't realize this meant so much to you," I said, and when I said it out loud, I realized how very little this election meant to me.

Anyway, after that heart-to-heart in the gents', McKelty and I rushed back to the assembly, where Emilé was just wrapping up her speech. Or should I say Emily. She had dropped the cool act completely and was giving an impassioned defence of her lizard sanctuary plan. She talked for at least five more minutes after I'd got back, and all of it was lizard-related.

As she left the lectern to the sound of one humanoid clapping, she undid the braids in her hair, popped down her collar and straightened her tie tight against her neck. She sat down next to Simone Green – the one person clapping – and Simone put her arm around my dorky little sister. It was all very weird.

McKelty was up next, and he was even worse than Emily. He resumed that hulking posture from before, the one where he places his hands flat on the lectern, and then proceeded to grumble at the audience for seven minutes. His speech was all about him being really great and therefore the right candidate, and, by my count, he said "join me in making Westbrook the Bestbrook" no less than five times. When he left the stage, it was so quiet that I heard a pigeon flapping its wings in the rafters.

"Well," Mr Joy said, taking the stage. "Very ... illuminating. Now, last but certainly not least, it's time for the final candidate. Boys and girls, put your hands together for Hank Zipzer, a young man of excellent taste who appreciates the finer things at this school. I want you to listen carefully to him. Hank, if you please."

I took the stage to thunderous applause. Everyone loved me, and I felt free and natural up on stage.

It was a shame that I was about to do what I was about to do.

"Quiet!" I bellowed. "Quieten down this instant!" I barked again and pounded the lectern. "I'm through playing the clown, and you should be too. This election has been a joke, but that stops now. This instant!" Then I paused and just glared at everyone with the evil eye. There were a few giggles from people who thought I was kidding, but I

kept glowering at the audience until I heard
that pigeon flapping its wings.

The little girl from yesterday started to
cry.

"That's better," I said. In the front row,
Frankie was anxiously shuffling through the
cue cards.

"I'm a serious candidate," I said. "So
have some respect for yourself and vote
for me. Because a vote for Hank Zipzer is
a vote for more homework, shorter break
times, a much longer school day, and
optimized database analytics." By the time
I had finished that sentence, the assembly
hall had gone from funeral quiet to angry
muttering. I kept going, and the discontent
grew: kids were booing. Kids were hissing.
Kids were stamping their feet and shaking
their fists.

But I didn't care. Frankie looked at the
cue cards one last time, then tossed them
over his shoulder. And for the next five

minutes or so, I talked over the angry din, explaining my plan. It was basically Emily's original campaign platform. I ended my tirade with an impassioned defence of Chef Anton's menu. Then I left the stage to thunderous boos and threats. I put my hand behind my ear like I couldn't hear it, smiling like a pro wrestler. The whole place actually started to shake.

Frankie and Ashley had to rush me away to a secure location under the cover of their school blazers. Kids were throwing two-day-old farfalle balls, aiming for my head.

# CHAPTER TWENTY-FIVE

"So..." Ashley began, once we'd got to an empty hallway corner. "You kind of went a little off-message there, Hank."

"It was the pictures on the cue cards, right?" Frankie said. "I told you I should have drawn them."

Ashley grabbed my face with both hands and examined my eyes. "Did you get a personality-changing brain virus?"

"I can't believe this!" Frankie started pacing. "Now McKelty is going to make school a hundred times worse."

"Nah," I said. "He doesn't want to change things. He just wants to get on the school council so his dad will like him. It's pretty sad, actually."

The whole school voted at lunchtime, and by lunchtime on Friday – sunflower and saffron soup, served chilled – the results were posted on the bulletin board. Emily got three votes: mine, hers and Simone Green's. I got one vote, which meant that either Frankie or Ashley didn't vote for me, though both swore otherwise. Thanks, guys.

McKelty won a landslide with a whopping fifteen votes. It seems that almost everyone in school chose not to exercise their democratic right.

I ran into McKelty by the bulletin board. He was carefully adding a zero to his vote total.

"Congrats, McKelty," I said and stuck out my hand. "Put it there, councillor."

He looked at my hand and smirked. "How

does it feel to be a loser, Zipzer? Actually, you don't know what it feels like *not* to be a loser."

"So, I hope your dad's proud of you now," I said, pretending not to hear him.

"Pfft," he snorted. "You fell for that? That was all an act. You've got a lot to learn about politics, loser."

I looked into his eyes. McKelty kept up his pose, bouncing and smirking, but I kept up my truth-stare, and the longer I stared at him, the more I knew that this was all an act, and he knew that I knew.

Just as I was about to shake my head and walk away, Miss Adolf approached from behind.

"Ah, I've been looking for you, Nicholas," she said. "Congratulations. See you tomorrow, eight o'clock sharp."

"Huh?" McKelty croaked. "Tomorrow is Saturday!"

"Yes. For the school council meeting, of

course. It's all here in your list of duties."
She handed him a sheet of paper filled with
words – on both sides.

"So I'll see you tomorrow, then," Miss
Adolf said. "In full school uniform."

"Saturday?" he repeated, weakly, and I
could see the doom in his eyes.

"Yes," Miss Adolf said. "Every Saturday
from 8 a.m. to 2 p.m!"

Miss Adolf marched away, but McKelty
was paralyzed.

As for me, I went home and played
Digging for Gold. I'd earned it. I kept playing
that evening till I beat the game. Actually,
you can't ever really beat the game. But
I got enough gold to the buy the game's
single best shovel: Blackbeard's Scourging
Inferno.

I didn't play Digging for Gold on Saturday;
I found a new game called Pop It 2 Stop
It. It's amazing. The object of the game is
to pop lots of balloons floating around the

screen, and when you get one it makes a
perfect popping sound.

When you pop them all, there's a long
moment when you can just sit back and watch
the blue sky and white clouds passing by.

# THE COLOSSAL
# CAMERA CALAMITY

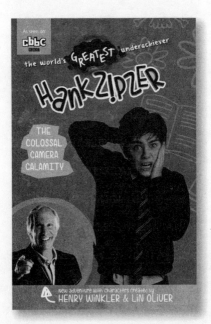

Hank hates school photos. No matter what he
does, he always ends up looking like he's just
seen Miss Adolf dancing. Bleurgh! This year,
he's determined to get it right. Unfortunately,
school bully Nick McKelty has other ideas...

# THE COW POO
# TREASURE HUNT

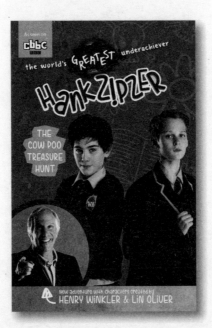

At Westbrook Academy, the school camping trips are legendary for all the wrong reasons. This year Hank is teamed up with his nemesis, McKelty. A leaky tent, a treasure hunt in a field of cowpats and Nick McKelty – can life get any worse?!